For Philip, Neil, and Elizabeth

First published in the United States 1992
by Dial Books for Young Readers
A Division of Penguin Books USA Inc.
375 Hudson Street
New York, New York 10014
Published in Great Britain 1991
by Simon and Schuster Young Books
Copyright © 1991 by John Talbot
All rights reserved
Printed in Belgium
First Edition
1 3 5 7 9 10 8 6 4 2

Library of Congress Cataloging in Publication Data
Talbot, John, 1948–
Pins and needles / written and illustrated by John Talbot—1st ed.
p. cm.
Summary: Feeling a tingly "pins-and-needles" sensation in his
trunk from having slept on it all night, Jean Pierre the elephant
tries different remedies to cure himself.
ISBN 0-8037-0942-0
[1. Elephants—Fiction.] I. Title.
PZ7.T145Pi 1992 [E]—dc20 91-13317 CIP AC

JJ FIC

PINS AND NEEDLES

John Talbot

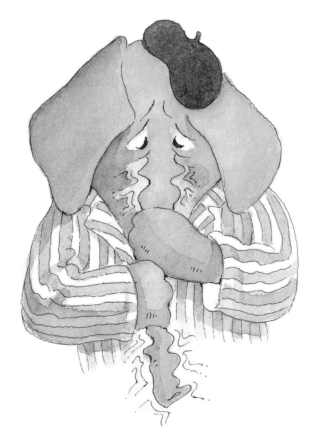

Dial Books for Young Readers

NEW YORK

As always Jean Pierre had slept very well, but when his alarm clock went off this morning he felt very uncomfortable.

"Ooooh," he groaned.

"What's the matter?" asked Bonsoir, his little friend.

Jean Pierre had slept all night on his trunk and now it felt very strange, as though there were pins and needles in it.

"Is there anything I can do?" inquired Bonsoir helpfully.

"No, my friend," said Jean Pierre.

"This is an elephant-sized problem."

Jean Pierre tried everything he could to get rid of the tingling feeling in his trunk.

He squeezed it.
He ran it under cold water.
He swung it around his head.

But nothing seemed to work.
He still had pins and needles.

Jean Pierre called his sister, Melissa.

"I've got pins and needles in my trunk," he said, "and they won't go away."

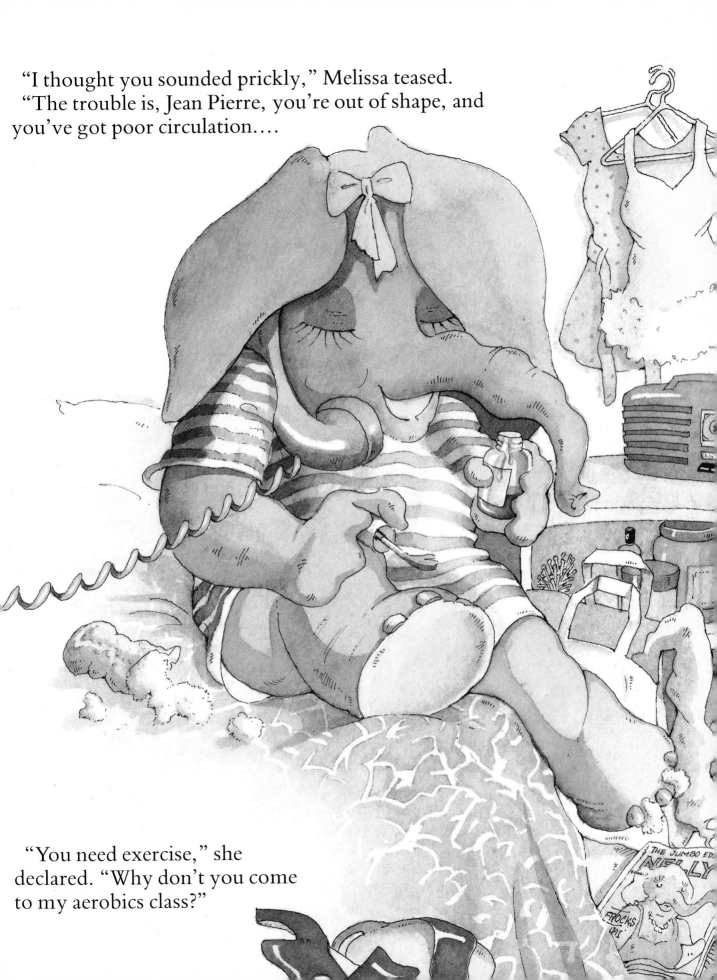

"I thought you sounded prickly," Melissa teased.
"The trouble is, Jean Pierre, you're out of shape, and
you've got poor circulation….

"You need exercise," she
declared. "Why don't you come
to my aerobics class?"

So Jean Pierre did, and Melissa was right.
He *was* out of shape.
    After the warm-up they went for a swim....

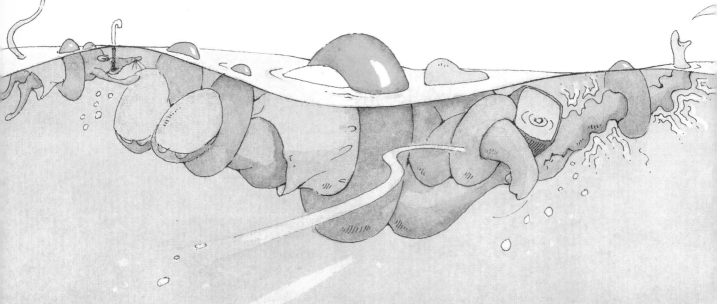

But after the swim he still had pins and needles.

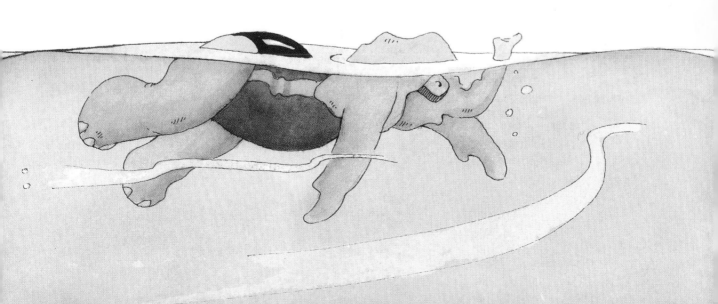

And after the weight lifting he still had pins and needles.

And after the cycling he still had pins and needles.

After all his hard work he was getting nowhere fast.
And he *still* had pins and needles.

So Jean Pierre
decided to get on his
bicycle and go visit his
Uncle Maurice, the inventor.
Perhaps he could help.

"Pins and needles, eh?"
said Uncle Maurice thoughtfully.
"Well, I've got just the thing.

"This magnet should draw out all your pins
and needles," he said. "It attracts metal and it's
the largest one I have."
  "It's not working," muttered Jean Pierre
twenty minutes later. "I still have
pins and needles."

"Why don't I pump some air into your trunk?"
suggested Uncle Maurice. "That should blow
out all the pins and needles."

Uncle Maurice led Jean Pierre
a safe distance away from anything hard.
"Here we go," he said as he let go
of Jean Pierre's trunk.

And Jean Pierre blew.
"Something's happening," said Uncle Maurice.

Something *was* happening ... but it didn't get rid of Jean Pierre's pins and needles.

"Maybe a little shock will do it," said Uncle Maurice, getting out his car battery. "If I attach both of these alligator clips to the end of your trunk—"

But Jean Pierre didn't wait to find out.

It was getting dark as he cycled away.

Back home he was quite exhausted, but he still had pins and needles. "I'll never get any sleep tonight," he yawned.

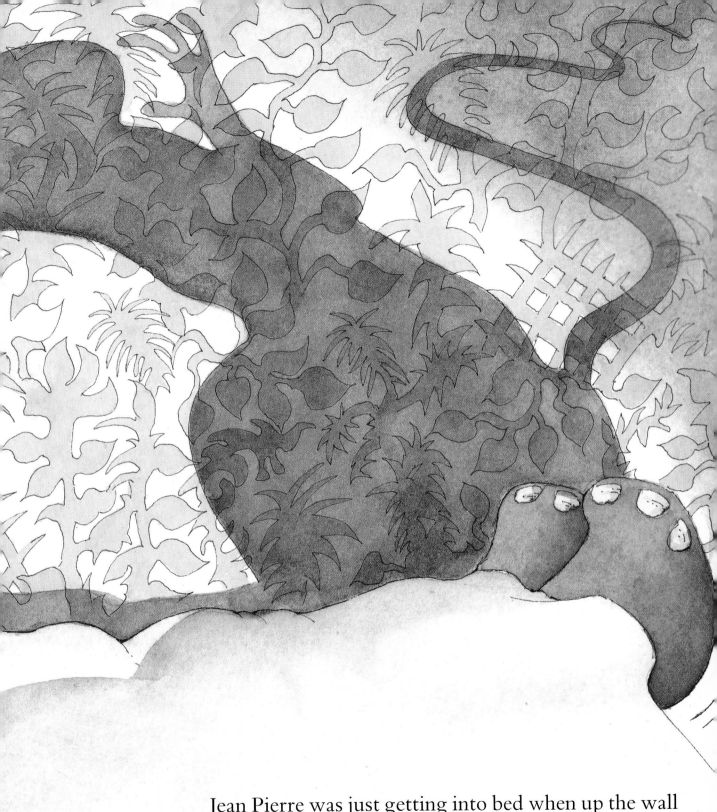

Jean Pierre was just getting into bed when up the wall
and over the ceiling a huge monster came lurching and
snarling toward him.
"Eeeeeek!" he shrieked,
and dove under the covers.

"It's only me," he heard a tiny voice say.
Slowly, Jean Pierre poked his head out.
There was his little friend, Bonsoir.
  "You gave me a terrible shock," said Jean Pierre.
  "Sorry," said Bonsoir. "But how does your
trunk feel now?"

"Fine," said Jean Pierre, surprised.
  "Absolutely FINE! My pins and needles
    are gone!"

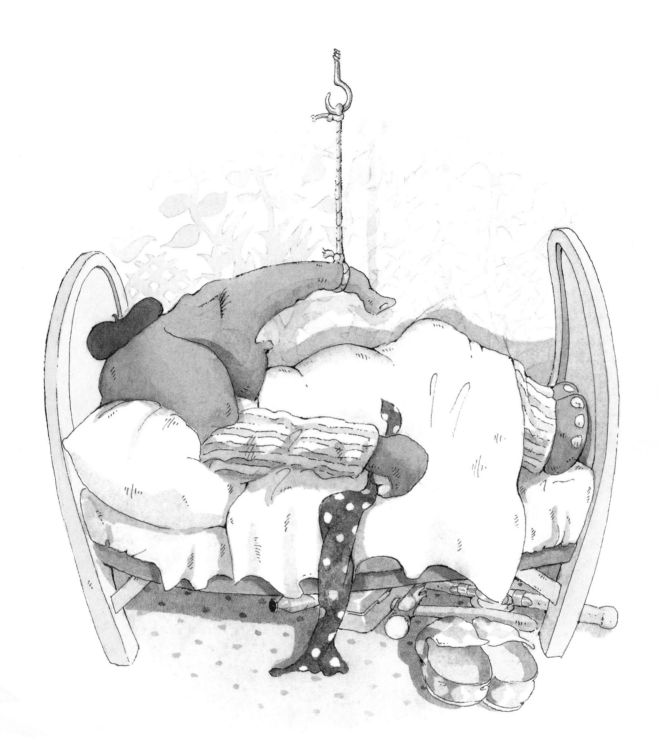

That night Jean Pierre slept very well.
And he never had pins and needles in his trunk again …
thanks to another one of Bonsoir's little ideas.